Tiger Tales

Almost True Animal Stories from Old Singapore

By Joyceline See Tully
Illustrations by Chloe Chang

Published by Pepper Dog Press Pte Ltd

Edited by Sim Ee Waun
Designed by Ann Neo

ISBN 978-981-14-8361-5
Second print run
Printing 2020 & 2022

Printed in Singapore

For Dave and our daughter Domi,
whose first love is animals.
— Joy

For the newest addition to the family Noelle, I hope
you will enjoy reading these stories some day.
— Chloe

&

Special thanks to our editor Ee Waun

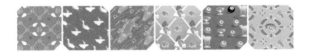

Author's Note

History is full of amazing stories and, indeed, that of Singapore is one born of the most fertile imagination, rich with romantic stories of sultans and adventurers and incredible animal tales.

The latter should come as no surprise. For much of its early history, Singapore was covered with lush rainforests filled with giant trees and exotic flora and fauna. Many creatures large and small called it home. If you had lived on the island then, you might have spotted giant red flying squirrels gliding by or danced to a sweet symphony of bird song on balmy jungle evenings.

With time and modernisation, some of these animals have disappeared from Singapore. Others are endangered. Environmental groups and champions of biodiversity are working hard to protect them, for if they die, there will be no more. With their passing, a little piece of old Singapore will disappear too.

It is with this in mind that I first started work on *Tiger Tales*, a collection of animal stories from early Singapore. The hope is to bring our collective memory of old Singapore to life for a very special audience—our young readers. While some poetic licence was taken in their telling, all of the stories featured in these pages are rooted in actual documented historical events.

Of course, how people at that time regarded and treated animals—often with both fascination and fear—is very different from how we see the natural world. These days, far from capturing or killing animals, it is in fact our responsibility to care for and protect the animals that we share this planet with. Indeed, things were very different then, yet these stories also offer a precious glimpse of Singapore from long ago and the lives of the island's pioneers.

All the information and illustrations have been painstakingly researched. Alongside the main stories, there are also many details in these pages that point to yet more stories of other creatures that share this island with us. Find more intriguing animal tales and animal-inspired craft and projects for littles ones on our website bit.ly/PepperDogPress or scan the QR code below.

I hope these pages will inspire our young readers to look beyond our concrete jungle, discover more of Singapore and uncover its fascinating stories.

— Joy

Contents

08
Lion City

22
A Rather Curious Creature

32
Oh, Rats!

42
The Dog & The Croc

54

A Rain
of Fish

62

A
Menagerie
in the
Garden

74

The Tiger at
The Raffles

90

Wild
at Heart

Lion City

Once upon a time, there was a prince from Palembang called Sang Nila Utama. Like many young men and women, he loved adventure. And one day, he got exactly that—a big adventure.

It was a bright, sunny morning with clear skies. The young prince was hunting and he was happy, for he loved being in the jungle. Suddenly he spotted a deer in the distance.

Without a thought, the prince ran after the animal. Before long, he found himself on a little hill. The deer had disappeared, but before him was a glittering stretch of sea.

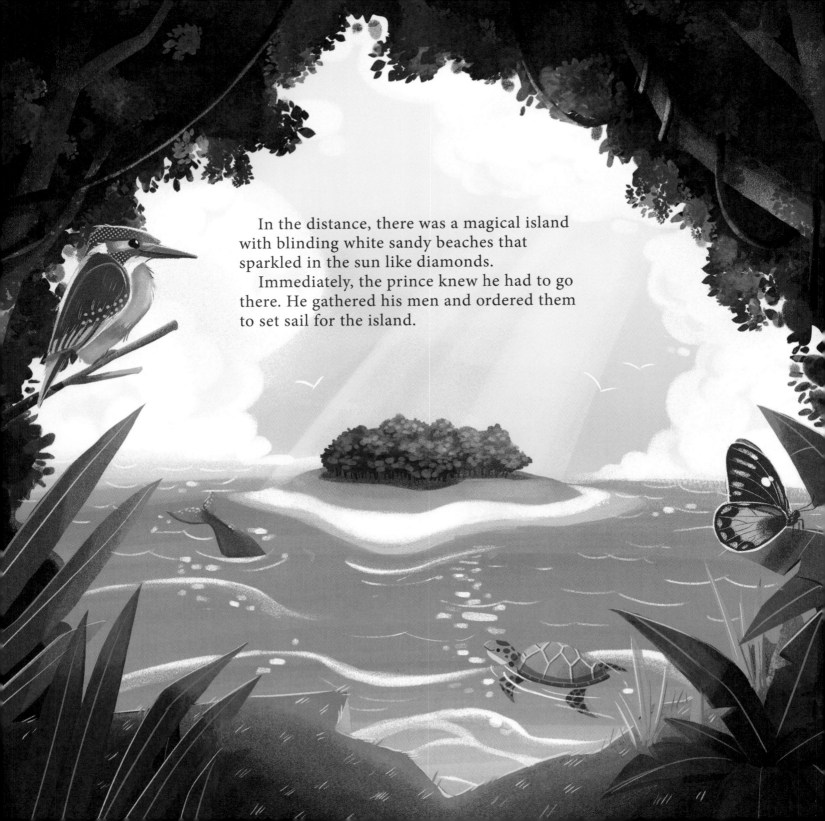

In the distance, there was a magical island with blinding white sandy beaches that sparkled in the sun like diamonds.

Immediately, the prince knew he had to go there. He gathered his men and ordered them to set sail for the island.

But the gods were not kind. The skies soon darkened and roared with thunder. Waves rose like watery giants, tossing the boat like a toy. Strong winds howled. "Oooooooooo.... Oooooooo..."

For the first time, the young prince was frightened. He wanted to go home.

"Appease the gods!" the captain shouted.
"Appease the gods," his men echoed.
Appease the gods, the young prince thought.
So he took the golden crown from his head and threw it into the sea.
Immediately, the waters grew calm. The dark clouds parted and the winds died down. In the distance, the island with white beaches appeared again like magic.

It's beautiful, the prince thought when he finally set foot on the island. The sand was white and soft under his feet. The rest of the island was jungle—green and wild and lush.

Chirp, chirp, chirp. Cicadas sang, while macaques swung from tree to tree. Woosh, woosh, woosh.

KU-OO!

Swish, swish, swish. Giant red squirrels glided gracefully by. Shhhhh. A mousedeer peeped from the bushes. Cheep, cheep, cheep. Rainbow-coloured birds twittered and chattered. The jungle was alive.

Just then, from the corner of his eye, Sang Nila Utama spotted a
sudden, quick movement in the tangled undergrowth. He grabbed his
spear and inched slowly, beckoning his men to follow.
　Swish, swash, swish. They heard rustling in the bushes ahead.
　Swish, swash, swish. There it was again—this time from under the tree.
　A hunt! The prince thought excitedly. They all crept forward.
Then suddenly…

"GRRRRRRRR, GRRRRRRRR, GRRRRRRRRR."
Everyone stopped. The men quietly drew their arrows and spears and they waited. No one made a sound.
    The prince looked long and hard. He signalled his men to stop while he padded ahead, his eyes darting and alert.

Circa 1290s

Then suddenly—swish swish SWASH!
Something big, black and red leapt out and almost
knocked the prince once over. But in a blink, it was gone.
All they saw was a huge blurry shape bounding away.

"What was that?" Sang Nila Utama exclaimed.
"Ah," said the oldest and wisest among his men.
"It was a lion, Your Majesty."
The prince and his men spent the rest of the day
searching, but the mysterious animal had disappeared.

And so, Sang Nila Utama named the island after his mystery beast. He called it Singapura, which means Lion City.

Sang Nila Utama loved the island so much, he stayed on and became the first king of Singapura. And that was how Singapore came to be.

Did the prince really see a lion? No one knows.

There have, however, been many sightings of another big cat in Singapore. But that is a story for another time.

DID YOU KNOW?

Sang Nila Utama was more than just legend. He was a real-life Palembang prince who lived in the 1300s. The white sand beaches of Singapura he spotted were real too. Archaeologists in the present day found brilliant white sand under the Padang and around Beach Road, which was once where the beach stood.

A Rather Curious Creature

Once upon a time, there was a Chinese admiral called Zheng He. He was a great explorer and adventurer. He sailed around the world in big ships to see new things, find new lands and meet new people.

On one of his trips to our part of the world, Zheng He and his men spotted a rather curious creature.

No one knew what it was.

Circa 1400s

They scratched their heads and muttered to each other. They looked at the animal up and down, and down and up. They pored over their books from front to back, and back to front.

Finally, they decided they would ask the people in the village.

KU-OO?

23

Zheng He gathered the villagers. "Name me the animal that is black and white, and big and fat," he said.

Is it the ZEBRA? The villagers asked. Or is it the SKUNK?

No, no, no! It isn't the zebra and it isn't the skunk, Zheng He and his men answered.

It is black and it is white, but it is not a zebra and not a skunk.

Is it a PANDA? The villagers replied. Or is it a PENGUIN?

No, no, no! Zheng He and his men shook their heads.
It is big and it is fat, but it is not a panda and not a penguin.
The villagers were puzzled.
What is this curious creature?
It has three toes on its two back legs, Zheng He said,
and four on its two front ones.

It has short fine hair, black in the back and front,
and white and smooth down the middle.
It is cute like a pig, with a snout longer than a pig's.
And it has a short stubby tail, but not at all like a pig's.

"Ahhhh," the villagers nodded knowingly.
The crowd parted and a little girl ran up.
 "It's his mummy!" she announced, holding forth a small bundle.
The animal was shaped exactly as Zheng He had described—
except it had little white stripes on a silky black coat.

Zheng He and his men scratched their heads and muttered to each other. They looked at the animal up and down, and down and up. Finally they shook their heads and said, "That's not it."

"Ahhhh," the villagers smiled knowingly.

The crowd parted and a little boy ran up.

"This is his mummy!" he announced, tugging an animal behind him.

It was black and white, but not a zebra and not a skunk.
It was big and fat, but not a panda and not a penguin.
It had three toes on its two back legs and four toes on
its two front ones.
It had short fine hair, black in the back and front,
and white and smooth down the middle.
It was cute like a pig, with a snout longer than a pig's.
And it had a short stubby tail, but not at all like a pig's.

Zheng He and his men looked at the animal up and down, and down and up. Finally they nodded and clapped their hands. "That is it!"

The villagers laughed and the children giggled. Zheng He and his men cheered and celebrated. The baby and its mummy were reunited. Now can you name this mysterious creature?

It is a **TAPIR**!

DID YOU KNOW?

This story is inspired by Zheng He and his encounter with the tapir in Southeast Asia during his travels in the 1400s. The Chinese called it the Divine Stag, or 神鹿. But clearly it looked more like a pig and not a stag, which is a male deer.

Four hundred years later, William Farquhar, the first Resident of Singapore became the first Westerner to study and describe the Malayan tapir. Farquhar even had a baby tapir for a pet! It was said that his pet tapir was gentle and ate from the breakfast table. And it loved cake. Imagine that!

Although rare, tapirs have been sighted in Singapore. It was seen in Pulau Ubin in the 1980s, and more recently in Changi in 2016.

Oh, Rats!

When the British first came to the island of Singapore, they found that it was home to exotic wild animals like leopards, pangolins and even deer that bark. They also discovered that there were lots of creepy crawlies like snakes and centipedes—and yes, rats!

In fact, Colonel William Farquhar, who was the first British put in charge of the island, had to deal with an infestation of rats. Big, fat, pesky rats.

Circa 1820

It started with just a few of them.
They were spotted here and there, in the
villages and the docks. Soon, there were more.
And more. And more.

They scampered here, they scurried there,
They turned up everywhere.
Some were grey and fat.
Some were skinny and black.
But all were as bold as brats.

They bullied the cats and bit the mats.
They chewed rice sacks and made off with snacks.
They marched into houses, they fought with street cats.
All were afraid of the nasty rats.

And the children chanted,
"One little ratty, two little ratty,
Three little ratty, four,
Five little ratty, six little ratty,
Seven little ratty. MORE!"

Soon all the houses in Singapore were filled with rats. The people were upset and frightened of these bold black rodents that snuck up on them in the day and tripped them over in the night. They wanted William Farquhar to do something about it.

So Colonel Farquhar came up with a plan.

"To anyone who kills a rat, I will give one wang," he declared.

The people heard and the people listened.
They made clever traps for the wily rodents.
There were cage traps and spring traps,
And traps with running nooses.
Soon, rats were brought to Colonel Farquhar
By the hundreds and the thousands.

But after a week, there were still far too many rats. They scampered here, they scurried there, they turned up everywhere.

So Colonel Farquhar said, "To anyone who kills a rat, I will give five duit!"

The people heard and the people listened.
They made clever traps for the wily rodents.
There were pincer traps and traps with doors,
And traps lined with lime and poison.
But weeks passed, and still, the rats were brought in
By the hundreds and the thousands.

The Colonel could not understand it. He stared at the rats and scratched his head. These rats looked strangely familiar, he thought. Were people bringing him the same dead rats day after day?

He had been tricked!

So Colonel Farquhar hatched a plan. He ordered his men to dig a deep pit. From then on, all the rats brought to him were buried in it.

Soon, there were fewer and fewer rats on the streets, in the houses and at the docks. Then the people stopped bringing him dead rats altogether. The Colonel's plan had worked! The rat infestation was over!

Now the children chanted,
"One little ratty, two little ratty,
Three little ratty, four,
Five little ratty, six little ratty,
Seven little ratty.
NO MORE!"

DID YOU KNOW?

William Farquhar was the First Resident of Singapore. He was appointed by the East India Company to help the British govern the island from 1819 to 1823.

During that time, Singapore faced many different pest infestations. In fact, soon after the rat problem, vicious centipedes overran Singapore. They dropped from the ceilings of houses and gave people nasty bites. Again, Farquhar offered people one wang, or a coin, for each centipede. Not to be tricked again this time, he made sure that they were buried immediately.

These stories were told to us by Singapore's very first storyteller Munshi Abdullah, who knew Farquhar personally and witnessed these events with his very own eyes.

The Dog
& The Croc

A crocodile is not a very good-looking animal, but it is a very powerful one.

It has bumpy, nubby skin, huge snapping jaws and sharp, frightful teeth. It has short stubby legs that can run faster than you or me, and it can smell its dinner from far, far away. When it is very, very hungry, it can swallow a dog or even a man whole.

Did you know that over a hundred years ago, there were crocodiles in Singapore? And if you were not careful, you might just meet one out and about.

This is a story about one such unlucky little dog who met a crocodile. However, the crocodile proved equally unfortunate when it won one fight but lost another.

Of the world's sixteen species of crocodiles, the largest is the saltwater crocodile. You could find them in the rivers and beaches of Singapore a long time ago. They are endangered now, but you can still spot them sunning themselves at the Sungei Buloh Wetlands.

It was a hot sunny morning with blue skies overhead and adventure in the air. Colonel William Farquhar—the very same one who loved tapirs—had been stuck indoors reading letters from his bosses far away in India. It was not a terribly exciting way to spend the morning and, in fact, rather dull.

Colonel Farquhar decided he needed some fresh air. So he put on his hat, straightened his sarong and took his faithful old dog out for a walk.

Raffy was a street dog, but a very well-behaved one. That day, old Raffy was in a frisky mood. He bounced ahead like a young pup, sniffing here, sniffing there, sniffing everywhere. Chasing birds and butterflies and everything in sight, he soon left his master far behind.

Before long, Raffy found himself by a river. The sight of the cool water made the old street dog very excited.

So splish, splash, splosh. He padded happily in.
But splish, splash, snap. There was a grin, a din and a spin.
Old Raffy was nowhere to be seen.

Ku-oo!

Now everyone knew that the waters between Singapore and Johor were infested with crocodiles. But very few people on the island had actually seen one in town—until that day.

Two young boys were playing on the riverbank when old Raffy went bounding in. They turned around just in time to see the long powerful jaws of a crocodile snap shut.

"Buaya! Buaya!" the two boys shouted as they scampered away.

Circa 1820s

News of the crocodile spread quickly and soon reached the Colonel, who was wondering where his pet had gone.

But splish, splash, snap. Dear Raffy was not seen since.

When Colonel Farquhar realised that a crocodile had eaten his dog, he was very sad and angry. But he was also very worried. What if the crocodile attacked the villagers and their children? Immediately, he ordered his men to drain the river and capture the crocodile.

Buaya means crocodile in Malay.

It took thirty men all morning and afternoon to build a small dam. They carried heavy logs and dropped big rocks into the narrowest part of the river. When all the water finally drained away, lo and behold! They saw a crocodile lounging in the thick mud.

It had cold beady eyes and dark leathery skin and a powerful tail that swung lazily from side to side. It was as long as four grown men laid head to toe on the ground and as heavy as forty. It was a giant crocodile. And its tummy was bulging with its breakfast.

"Attack!" the Colonel ordered.

Immediately, thirty spears flew at the crocodile, but they fell away as if by magic. The animal didn't move but merely glared at the crowd.

Another thirty spears flew. Again, they fell harmlessly to the ground.

The men looked at each other in wonder. Did the crocodile have magical powers?

They released their spears again. This time, many pierced the creature's tough leathery hide. The crocodile heaved itself on its short legs and took a few steps towards the men. Then it staggered and collapsed.

The crowd gave a sigh of relief.

"Hurray! Hurray!" they cheered.

To warn the people about the dangers that might lurk in the river, Colonel Farquhar ordered his men to hang the crocodile from the jawi-jawi tree down the road. It took ten men to move the giant crocodile from the bottom of the riverbed and another twenty to hang it from the tree.

Everyone came to see the giant creature, which looked impressive even when dead.

But… splish, splash, snap…

Poor Raffy was seen no more.

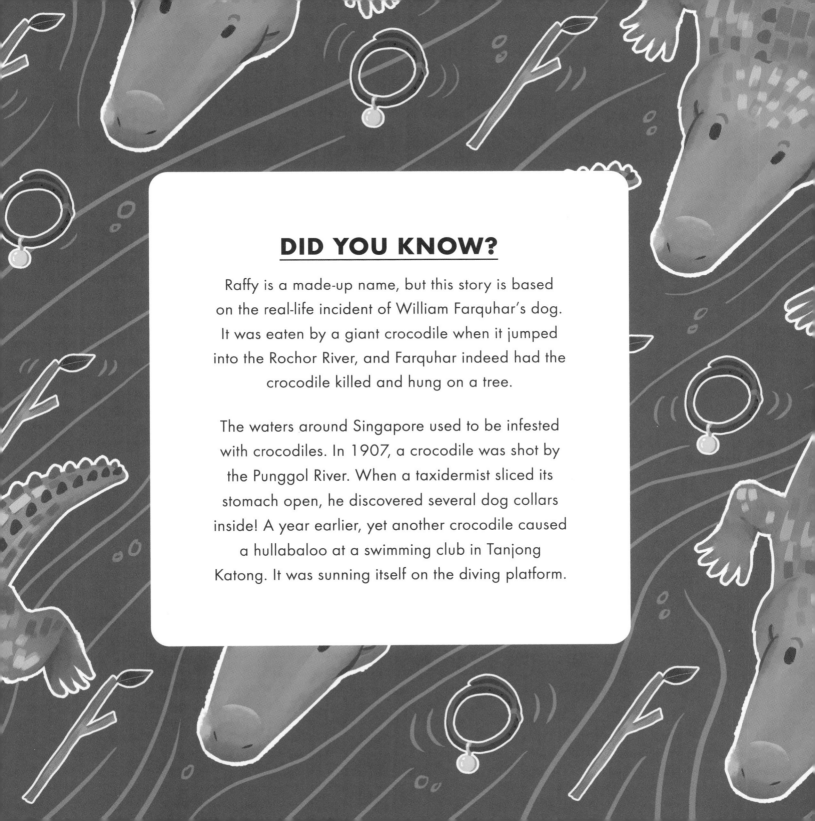

DID YOU KNOW?

Raffy is a made-up name, but this story is based on the real-life incident of William Farquhar's dog. It was eaten by a giant crocodile when it jumped into the Rochor River, and Farquhar indeed had the crocodile killed and hung on a tree.

The waters around Singapore used to be infested with crocodiles. In 1907, a crocodile was shot by the Punggol River. When a taxidermist sliced its stomach open, he discovered several dog collars inside! A year earlier, yet another crocodile caused a hullabaloo at a swimming club in Tanjong Katong. It was sunning itself on the diving platform.

A Rain of Fish

More than a hundred and fifty years ago, there was an earthquake in Sumatra, a big island that lay not far from Singapore.

It happened one evening when the people were getting ready for bed. Without warning, the ground suddenly moved and shook. Deep cracks opened, swallowing trees and houses and animals. Many people and animals were killed.

The earthquake was so powerful that people who lived far away felt it too. Even the villagers on the island of Singapore, which was days away by boat, felt the earth move.

MALAYA

SINGAPORE

SUMATRA

Seven-year-old Ah Huat was fetching water from the well when he felt the ground rumbling under his feet. Now, Ah Huat did not know about Sumatra or the earthquake that was happening there.

He thought he was faint from hunger until he heard someone cry, "Earthquake! Earthquake!"

Ah Huat looked up and saw the houses shaking. Around him, the villagers screamed while the animals barked, howled and screeched. Everyone was frightened. Was the world ending? No one in Singapore had ever felt an earthquake before.

After a while, the tremors stopped. But it was not over yet. Giant claps of thunder and flashes of lightning lit up the sky. Then it rained for three days and three nights over the island of Singapore.

Ah Huat stayed at home with his family, but that did not keep him very dry at all. The roof leaked badly and everything got damp.

Outside, the ground turned muddy and gooey. On the third day, the rain finally stopped.

When Ah Huat and the villagers came out of their houses, they were greeted by an incredible sight. There were fish in muddy pools on the ground everywhere.

Small fish, big fish. Dead fish, live fish!

The earthquake had brought a rain of fish, the villagers declared excitedly to each other! Everyone got out their buckets and down on their knees to catch the fish.

For the rest of the week, Ah Huat's mother cooked fried fish. They were the best meals he ever had.

From then on, every time there was thunder and lightning, the villagers remembered the earthquake in Singapore and the rain of fish that followed. There have been many earthquakes in the region since, but none has brought a rain of fish to Singapore again.

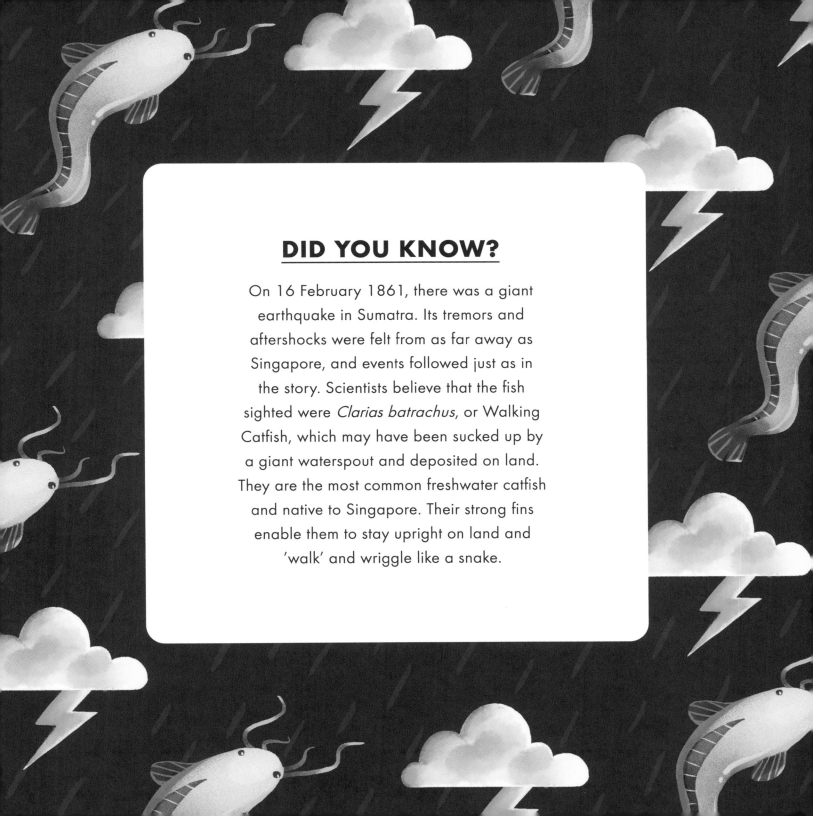

DID YOU KNOW?

On 16 February 1861, there was a giant earthquake in Sumatra. Its tremors and aftershocks were felt from as far away as Singapore, and events followed just as in the story. Scientists believe that the fish sighted were *Clarias batrachus*, or Walking Catfish, which may have been sucked up by a giant waterspout and deposited on land. They are the most common freshwater catfish and native to Singapore. Their strong fins enable them to stay upright on land and 'walk' and wriggle like a snake.

A Menagerie in the Garden

Once upon a time, a garden could be more than just a garden. It could be a zoo too. And so it was with Singapore's first Botanic Gardens.

It was created one hundred and fifty years ago, when the island was still wild and forested, and people travelled in bullock carts.

KU-OO!

Some wanted Singapore to have a beautiful public garden that everyone could enjoy, so they bought land from a very rich man called Hoo Ah Kay to make one. They called it the Botanic Gardens, and it stood in the same spot in Tanglin as we know it today.

Circa 1875

In those early days, the gardens had more than just trees and flowers, swans and terrapins. It also had animals big and small—more than one hundred and forty of them, such as kangaroos, an emu, a wallaby and even some orang utan.

It all started with Waja, a female Sumatran rhinoceros.

She was a gift from a very important man, the Governor of the Straits Settlements. She had two stubby horns at the front of her head and she weighed as much as forty small children.

Waja was very gentle, but a little noisy. She would grunt and pant and squeal and squeak. When she was hungry, she would squeak, quietly at first, then louder and louder until she was fed.

Ahmad, the garden boy found that out the first night she arrived.

It was a hot, sweaty evening. Ahmad had worked hard all day and now, he was looking forward to his dinner. Boiled sweet potatoes and some fresh cempedak—his favourite!

It had been an exciting day with the arrival of the giant beast his father called 'badak'. Ahmad was very impressed with the animal. It scared him a little too, but he wasn't going to tell anyone that.

Suddenly, there was a little squeak behind the bushes. The boy looked around nervously. "SQUEAK, SQUEAK."

He heard it again, this time louder and closer. Could it be the badak?

SQUEAK!

Badak means rhino in Malay.

Ahmad peered through the bushes and saw Waja laying on her side in a corner of her pen. "Phffffffff," she snorted through half-closed eyes. Ahmad moved closer to take a look.

"Phffffffff," went the rhino.

Ahmad moved closer still.

"Phffffffff," the rhino snorted again.

Ahmad moved even closer.

"PHFFFFFFFFFFFF!" Waja bellowed.

This time, Ahmad jumped and ran straight back to the bushes. But the poor boy soon realised that he had dropped his dinner! He inched his way back, peeked through the bushes and saw the rhino chomping down on sweet potatoes and cempedak.

When she finished, Waja turned towards Ahmad and gave a little snort, as if to say thank you. Then she moved to a corner of the pen and settled in for the night.

That was how Ahmad discovered she loved sweet potatoes and cempedak.
Another time, he brought her some sugar cane and she chomped it all down too.
And her favourite thing to do? Roll around and wallow in the mud!

Ahmad and the rhino became good friends. Sometimes, she would let Ahmad and his friends pet and stroke her, and eat from their hands.

In time, other animals joined Waja in the zoo in the garden. There was a young tiger, a gift from the Sultan of Trengganu. There were two spotty leopards, one from the King of Siam. There were two black panther cubs, which were cute and small but vicious, with sharp fangs and fierce snarls.

There were eagles and foxes and deer, and even a sloth bear that came all the way from Australia. There was a Malayan sun bear called Jelebu, who was gentle and sweet and gave children rides on his back, and Eva, the Malayan tapir who lived in the house of the Gardens' director and ate out of his hand.

There were snakes too, including pythons, cobras and green vipers. And there were monkeys— so many that they built a special house for them and called it Monkey House.

For taking such good care of Waja, Ahmad was eventually promoted to zookeeper and helped look after the animals for many years. But his favourite was always the Sumatran rhinoceros who loved sweet potatoes, cempedak and sugar cane!

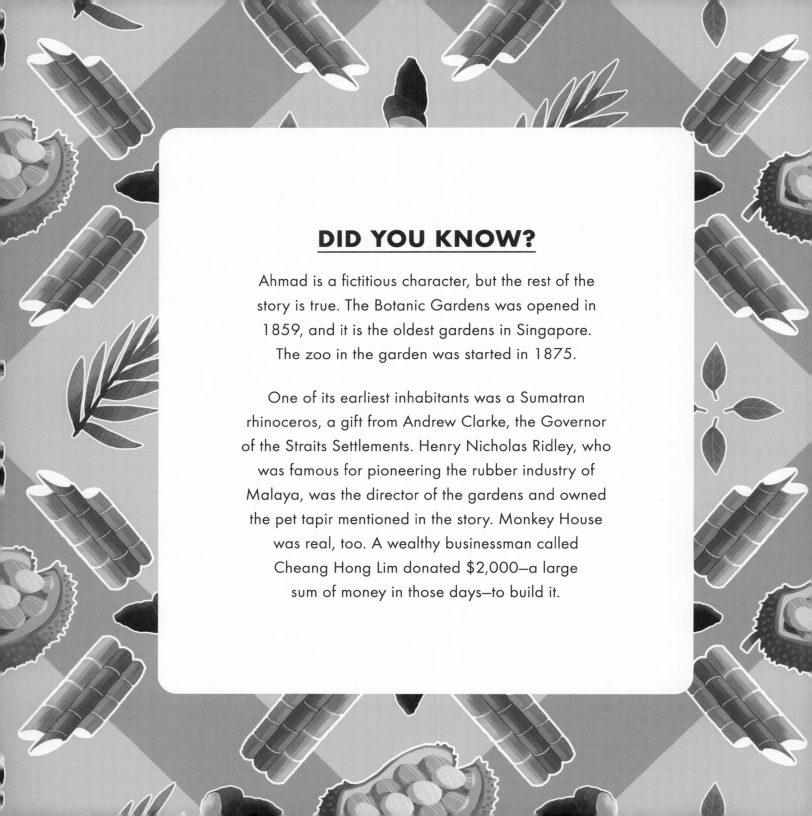

<u>DID YOU KNOW?</u>

Ahmad is a fictitious character, but the rest of the story is true. The Botanic Gardens was opened in 1859, and it is the oldest gardens in Singapore. The zoo in the garden was started in 1875.

One of its earliest inhabitants was a Sumatran rhinoceros, a gift from Andrew Clarke, the Governor of the Straits Settlements. Henry Nicholas Ridley, who was famous for pioneering the rubber industry of Malaya, was the director of the gardens and owned the pet tapir mentioned in the story. Monkey House was real, too. A wealthy businessman called Cheang Hong Lim donated $2,000—a large sum of money in those days—to build it.

As in the story, the Sumatran rhinoceros
loved sweet potatoes, cempedak and sugar cane.
When it died in August 1877, its skeleton was
donated to the then Raffles Museum for scientific
study. However, no one knows where it is today.

The Sumatran rhinoceros is now a critically
endangered species that is found only in Indonesia.
At last count in 2019, there are only about
eighty left in the world.

The zoo in the garden stayed open for more
than thirty years until it became too expensive to
feed the animals. When it closed, all the animals
were given away. Singapore's Botanic Gardens,
meanwhile, has flourished over the years.
In 2015, it was recognised as Singapore's
first UNESCO World Heritage Site.

The Tiger at The Raffles

A long, long time ago, Singapore was covered with jungle and filled with wild animals. There were pangolins, wild oxen, boars, mousedeer and more. But the king of the jungle were the tigers. They were strong and fierce, and everyone was afraid of them.

Luckily, the tigers mostly hunted in the jungles. Sometimes, they wandered out to where people lived—like the time a tiger visited the famous Raffles Hotel.

Circa 1902

It was almost dawn but most of the hotel guests were still in bed. Only a few staff were already hard at work, including eight-year-old Ali. He worked at the Bar & Billiard Room, where gentlemen gathered to read their newspapers, drink and have their dinner.

In those days, most people in Singapore were poor and it was not uncommon for children to go to work.

It was Ali's job to scrub the floors every morning. Scrubbing floors was tiring, but Ali was a tough little boy and quite an expert at it. First he dipped his cloth into a pail of soapy water, then he swished it around. Next he wrung the cloth dry before plopping it on the floor.

Dip, swish, wring and plop. Dip, swish, wring and plop. Dip, swish, wring…. GRRRRRR…..

What was that?
Ali's ears pricked up.
Was that his tummy growling?
He looked around nervously and scrubbed a bit faster.
Dip, swish, wring, plop.
Dip, swish, wring, plop.
Dip, swish, wring, GRRRRRRR...

What was that?
Ali looked up.

This time, he knew it was not his tummy.
"GRRRRRR ….."
Ali froze.
This time, it was loud and clear. Ali knew exactly what it was.
TIGER!
Beads of sweat ran down his forehead. He had heard people talk about tigers in the village, and Ali knew how dangerous they were.

Slowly, he crept towards the door, keeping as quiet as he could. As soon as he was out of the room, Ali ran, shouting at the top of his voice, "TIGER! TIGER! There's a TIGER in the room!"

By this time, the sun had risen and many hotel guests were awake. Hearing the commotion, a small crowd soon gathered outside the Bar & Billiard Room.

"There's a tiger."

"Oh my, a tiger?"

"Oh yes, a tiger."

"Oh no, a tiger!"

The crowd whispered and they muttered and they fidgeted.

"Call Mr Phillips!"

"Who's Mr Phillips?"

"Yes, Mr Phillips!"

"Where's Mr Phillips?"

BAR &
BILLIARD
ROOM

The crowd whispered and they muttered and they waited.
Finally, Mr Charles Phillips, school principal and expert gunman, strode in.
He was still in his pyjamas, but he had his trusty rifle in hand.
"Where is the tiger?" he asked in a booming voice, his moustache twitching in anticipation.

"GRRRRRRRRRRRR…..!" came the thundering reply.
Everyone turned pale with fear. Well, everyone except Mr Phillips,
who cocked his rifle and marched straight into the Bar & Billiard Room.
He looked under the billiard table. He looked behind the bar counter.
He looked inside the dining room. But there was no tiger in sight.

Suddenly he heard the sound of scratching under his feet.

"GRRRRRRRRRRR…."

The tiger was **under** the Bar & Billiard Room. You see, it was built on pillars raised above the ground which kept the room cool—with more than enough space for a tiger to hide.

"GRRRRRRRRRR…"

Mr Phillips rushed outside and got on all fours to look under the building. Squinting hard, he thought he saw something in the murky darkness.

"Bang! Bang! Bang!" he hurriedly fired three shots.
"RRRRRAAAAAAAAAAAAAAAAAHH!!!!"
He had missed! Now the tiger was angrier than ever.
Mr Phillips peered under the building again. This time he saw two shining eyes in the dark, and they were looking right back at him. It was the tiger!
Slowly, he raised his rifle and took careful aim. He was not going to miss again. He took a deep breath, pulled the trigger and fired.

"Bang! Bang!"
"RRRRAAAAAAAAAAAAAA!!!!!!"
A fierce, deafening roar shook the
building. There was loud thrashing
below the floorboards, as if the tiger was
clawing its way through the wood.

Everyone shuddered—except Mr Phillips.
He raised his gun one last time.
"Bang!"
He fired a last shot.
Everything fell silent. The crowd waited.
Minutes passed.
No one moved.

Finally, a few brave workers crawled in. When they pulled the animal out from underneath the building, they found a Bengal tiger.

It was as long as a crocodile and taller than a grown man. It had a golden coat with bold black stripes and shiny sharp teeth that glistened in the sun. It was most magnificent!

Everyone cheered loudly. They were safe now. Mr Phillips was a hero!

As for Ali, he was well rewarded for raising the alarm and he never forgot his close encounter for the rest of his life.

DID YOU KNOW?

Ali is a fictitious character, but the rest of the cast in this story are real, including the tiger which had escaped from a circus nearby. Mr Charles Phillips was the principal of Raffles Institution which stood opposite the Raffles Hotel then. An avid hunter, he shot the Bengal tiger at the Bar & Billiard Room at the Raffles Hotel in August 1902.

There were many tiger sightings in Singapore up until the 1930s, when the last wild tiger was shot in Choa Chu Kang.

Unlike then, tigers and other wild animals are protected these days. Hunting and trading in wildlife are now against the law in many countries.

There are many more animals which can be found in Singapore. They are hidden in the pages of this book. Can you find them?

Asian koel
Black-naped oriole
Blue pansy butterfly
Cabbage white butterfly
Catfish
Civet cat
Common birdwing butterfly
Common grass yellow butterfly
Dugong
Gold-ringed cat snake
Green crested lizard
Hornbill
Horseshoe crab
Kingfisher
Ladybird
Lesser grass blue butterfly
Long-tailed macaque
Malayan tapir
Mousedeer
Neon tetra
Orang utan
Otter
Purple climber crab
Red giant flying squirrel

Sambar deer
Sea turtle
Straw-headed bulbul
Sunda pangolin
White-spotted cat snake
Yellow-vented bulbul

WILD AT HEART

Singapore may be a small country, but it is home to a rich diversity of plants and animals. Meet some of the surprising inhabitants that call it home.

SUNDA PANGOLIN

With its short legs, long tail and a thick fat body covered in scales, the pangolin is often mistaken for a reptile. But it is actually a mammal. The Sunda pangolin is also called the Malayan Scaly Anteater, because like the anteater, its favourite foods are ants and termites. When attacked, the pangolin curls itself into a tight ball and uses the sharp scales on its tail to lash out.

The pangolin is nocturnal, which means it comes out to play and hunt at night. It is a very good climber and loves to spend time in the trees. You might spot it in forested areas like the Central Catchment Nature Reserve and Pulau Tekong.

MOUSEDEER

The mousedeer features in traditional Malay stories as a clever and crafty creature. There are two species of mousedeer in Singapore: the lesser mousedeer and the greater mousedeer. They both look like deer, but are much, much smaller in size.

The lesser mousedeer is less than fifty centimetres when fully grown and weighs under two kilograms—lighter than a newborn baby! It has startlingly skinny legs and a triangular white patch on its neck. Unlike the stag, the male mousedeer does not have antlers.

The lesser mousedeer lives in forested areas like the Central Catchment Nature Reserve and loves fruit and young leaves. The greater mousedeer, on the other hand, is far harder to spot. In fact, many people thought it had disappeared from Singapore until it was sighted in Pulau Ubin in 2009.

PALM CIVET

Although it is also called Civet Cat, the palm civet is not a cat. Instead, it is related to meerkats and mongooses. The palm civet is also nocturnal. It has a long tail, sleek body and short legs, with a long muzzle and a black patch over its eyes like a raccoon.

It loves mango, banana and the seed pods of the Rain Tree, but it also feeds on small birds, snakes and rats. In Singapore, the palm civet is also called Musang, which means fox in Malay. Some call it Toddy Cat, because it loves the palm tree sap that is used to make the drink called Toddy. It lives in forests, mangroves, parks and even in the roofs of houses.

STRAW-HEADED BULBUL

You can hear its sweet song in places like Bukit Timah Nature Reserve, Dairy Farm Nature Park and Pulau Ubin if you are lucky. Once widely found in Southeast Asia, this songbird is now critically endangered, thanks to poaching and the loss of the forests that make up its home. In fact, Singapore is one of the last places in the world where the straw-headed bulbul still thrives in the wild!

It has a yellowish-orange crown with black eyes and a brownish, dark green body, and it is the largest bulbul species in Singapore. While it is not much to look at, its song is melodious and rich, and usually heard at dawn or just before nightfall.

HORNBILL

Did you know that traders from all over the world once travelled to Singapore for hornbill casques in the 13th and 14th centuries? The casques—the bony hump on the upper part of the bird's bill—were traded as a precious commodity in exchange for goods like ceramic and jewels.

Unfortunately, hornbills are still being hunted illegally for their casques even today. The most valuable of all is the solid casque of the helmeted hornbill. This is why you will not find many helmeted hornbills around the world today. It is critically endangered and has been extinct in Singapore since 1950.

Instead, you are more likely to spot the Oriental pied hornbill on the island. A black and white bird with a distinctive pale yellow bill and a loud cackle, it had all but disappeared from our shores by the 1960s. But thanks to the Singapore Hornbill Project launched in 2004, it is now thriving here again. At over one metre long from bill to tail, the Oriental pied hornbill is one of Singapore's largest birds. Look out for them across the island, especially in the forested areas of Changi, Bukit Timah and on Pulau Ubin. Occasionally, they may even appear in your garden!

HORSESHOE CRAB

There are four types of horseshoe crabs in the world and two of them—the coastal horseshoe crab and the mangrove horseshoe crab—live in Singapore. You will find them mostly in the mudflats near mangrove swamps on the northern shores of the island.

This harmless creature has a long sharp tail which it uses to maneuver underwater and to flip itself upright when overturned. To eat, it bulldozes quietly in the mud and breaks up food with the pointy bits on its legs, then lets the food flow into its mouth. It likes clams, worms, algae and even dead creatures. Other interesting facts about the horseshoe crab—its blood is blue in colour and has special powers to detect bacteria.

But the horseshoe crab is not really a crab. Instead, it is more closely related to the spider and sea scorpion. Fully grown, it may only be the size of an adult's palm, but did you know that the horseshoe crab is as old as dinosaurs? It has been around for more than four hundred and fifty million years! For such a tiny animal, the horseshoe crab lives for a long time—up to thirty human years. Sadly, it is now endangered. It is often caught in fishing nets as by-catch and dies as a result. If you want to help protect our horseshoe crab population, volunteer with the Horseshoe Crab Rescue & Research programme by the Nature Society (Singapore).

SAMBAR DEER

You may not believe this, but Singapore is home to the sambar deer. At about one-and-a-half metres tall and weighing more than three hundred kilograms, it is the largest of Southeast Asian deer. But you will have to be very lucky to spot one here, for today, there are less than twenty of them on the island. They are likely scattered in the few thick forests left, like the Bukit Timah Nature Reserve.

The sambar deer eats mostly grass, shrubs and fruit. Another nocturnal animal, it likes to snooze during the day and play at night. The sambar deer is a good swimmer and likes to be near water.

OTTER

Otters were once thought to be extinct in Singapore. But these days, these cute playful mammals can be spotted in many parts of the island, from Sungei Buloh Wetland Reserve and Kranji in the north, to Bishan Park and Labrador Park. There has even been otter sightings in the Botanic Gardens and Gardens by the Bay!

There are two different species of otters in Singapore—the Asian small-clawed otter, which is small with little claws and a short flat snout, and the bigger, more common smooth-coated otter with its velvety coat.

Otters live in pairs or as a family. They are semi-aquatic: they live on land and are comfortable in both fresh and sea water. They love to hunt frogs, crabs, turtles and all types of fish, including pretty koi fish!

BANDED LEAF MONKEY

Also called the Raffles' Banded Langur, this is one of the two species of monkeys that call Singapore home. (The other is the long-tailed macaque.) There were once many of these black and white monkeys all over Singapore. They lived in Bukit Timah, Changi, Tampines and even Tuas. However, as more and more forests were turned into roads and buildings, many of these monkeys lost their home. Today, there are only about sixty of them left on the whole island, and they live mostly in the Central Catchment Nature Reserve.

The banded leaf monkey loves seeds, leaves and fruit, even the unripe ones. It also loves swinging from tree to tree, to tree. In fact, if it could, it would not come down to the ground!

ASIAN KOEL

With its blood-red eyes, the Asian koel is very distinctive and easily recognised. However, you are more likely to hear it than see it. It has a very loud, high-pitched call that goes "ku-ooo ku-ooo", often in the early hours of the morning.

The Asian koel does not have its own nest. Instead it lays its eggs in the nests of other birds, especially those of house crows. The baby koel will stay with its adopted family until it is grown and can fly.

The Asian koel can be found all over the island. Can you spot it in the pages of this book?

RED GIANT FLYING SQUIRREL

With a long furry tail that measures more than fifty centimetres, this is probably one of the largest flying squirrels in Southeast Asia. It comes out at night and loves to glide freely from tree to tree, sometimes up to a distance of a hundred metres!

Although it is called the Red Giant Flying Squirrel, it is not red in colour. Instead, it has dark brown fur on its back, an orange belly, a black snout and black feet. Sadly, it has not been seen in Singapore since the 1980s. The colugo, a smaller gliding mammal, is more common here and you can find them in the nature reserves of the Central Catchment area, clinging to tree trunks or gliding from tree to tree at dusk.

pepper dog press

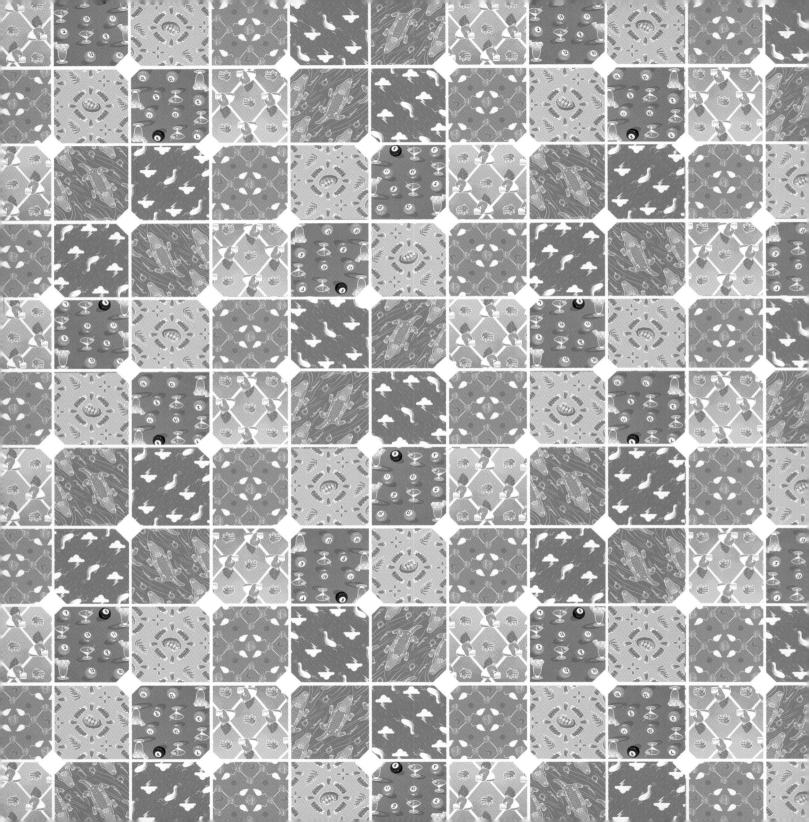